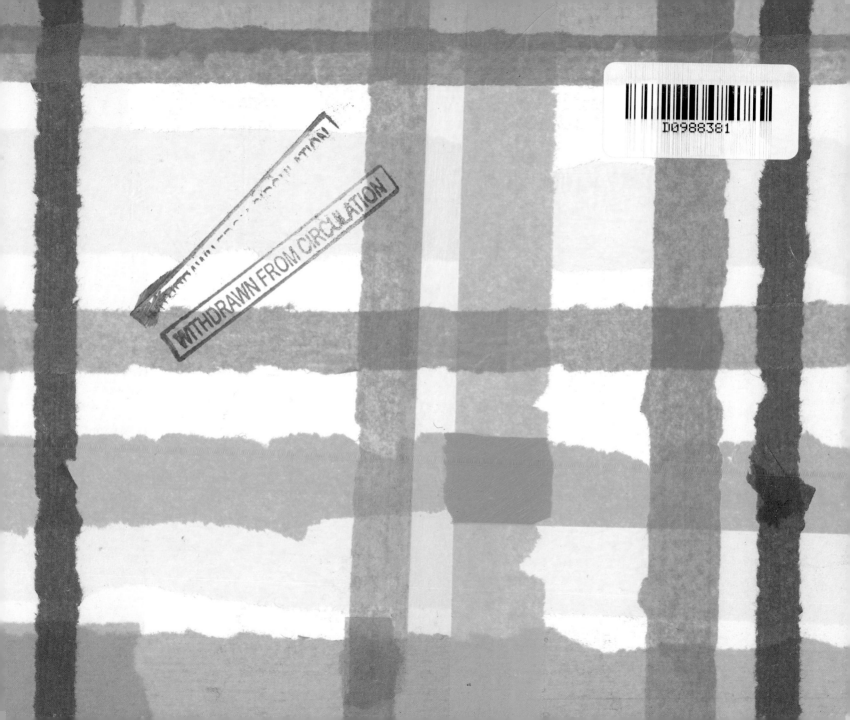

For Diana Cockerton
J.D.

For Lisa
C.T.

First published 1995 by Walker Books Ltd
87 Vauxhall Walk, London SE11 5HJ

This edition published 1996

2 4 6 8 10 9 7 5 3 1

Text © 1995 Joyce Dunbar
Illustrations © 1995 Carol Thompson

This book has been typeset in Garamond.

Printed in Hong Kong

British Library Cataloguing in Publication Data
A catalogue record for this book is available
from the British Library.

ISBN 0-7445-4719-9

OOPS-A-DAISY!

·AND OTHER TALES FOR TODDLERS·

Written by Joyce Dunbar   Illustrated by Carol Thompson

WALKER BOOKS

AND SUBSIDIARIES

LONDON · BOSTON · SYDNEY

OOPS-A-DAISY!

Sadie came to play.

"I can be upside down," said Sadie.

"So can I," I said.

"I can go head over heels," said Sadie.

"So can I," I said.

"I can wear my trousers inside out," said Sadie.

"So can I," I said.

"I can put my
jumper back to front,"
said Sadie.
"So can I," I said.

"Let's be back to back,"
said Sadie.
And we were.

"Let's be
    higgledy-piggledy,"
    said Sadie.
        And we were.

"Let's go oops-a-daisy," said Sadie. And we did. Sadie bumped her head on mine. I bumped my head on Sadie's.

"Ooow!" Sadie yowled.

"Ouch!" I howled.

"That was good fun, wasn't it?" said Sadie.
"Let's play it again," I said.

WHAT IF?

I went into the garden
with Grump.
We played "What if?"

"What if I sneezed,"
I said to Grump,
"and all the worms came
up and sneezed too?"

"That would be funny,"
said Grump.

"What if I danced," I said to Grump, "and all the mice came out and danced with me?"

"That would be funny," said Grump.

"What if I whistled," I said,
"and all the birds flew down
and whistled too?"

"You can't whistle,"
said Grump.

"I know I can't," I said.
"But I'll be able to whistle
one day ... and then
you never know
what might
happen."

NICKY COMES TO PLAY

"Nicky's coming to play today,"
said Mum. "Do you want
Nicky to come and play?"
"Yes," I said, "I do."

Nicky was shy when
he came.
He wouldn't
look.

I showed Nicky my toy truck. Then he looked.
Nicky wanted to play with my toy truck.
I gave it to him. He drove
it over the sofa.

I wanted the toy truck too.
I took it off him and gave him
my play dough machine.

Nicky made squiggly
things with the play
dough machine.

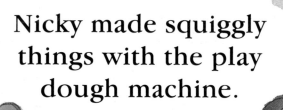

I wanted the play dough machine. I took it off him and gave him Grump to play with.

Nicky cuddled Grump.
Grump's mine
to cuddle.

I took Grump away from Nicky.
Nicky cried.

After that he went home. Now I had all
my toys to myself. I had my toy truck and
my play dough machine and Grump.

They didn't seem so much fun any more
so I went off and sucked my blanket.

I hope Nicky comes again soon.

THE BEST-DRESSED TED

"They're having a competition at the fête this year," said Mum. "Look, it's for the best-dressed teddy bear."

"Grump doesn't wear dresses," I said. "You're right," said Mum. "So let's make him some trousers instead."

She made him some spotted trousers

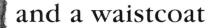

and a waistcoat

and some shoes.

I made him a hat.

He didn't look like Grump any more. He looked like some other bear.

We took him to the fête. There were hundreds of teddy bears, all dressed up. The judge looked at them all.

"You're looking very smart today," he said to Grump.
Grump just looked Grumpy.

He didn't win.
A bear in a sailor suit won.

I took Grump home.
I took off all his new clothes.
"You should have gone
without any clothes,"
I said, "then you
would have won."

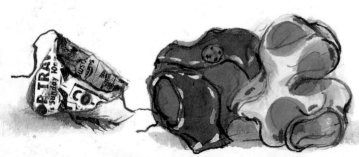

"Never mind. I'll give you a prize." And I gave him a great big hug.

MORE WALKER PAPERBACKS
For You to Enjoy

HERBERT: FIVE STORIES
by Ivor Cutler/Patrick Benson

Every morning when Herbert wakes up he's a different kind of animal – an elephant or a chicken, a kangaroo or a capybara! "Ivor Cutler has warmth, humour and genuine originality in spades and his Herbert is great." *Wendy Cope, The Sunday Telegraph*
0-7445-4778-4   £4.99

BLACKBOARD BEAR
by Martha Alexander

Four enchanting stories about a boy and his magical chalked bear companion.
"Charming and appealing… Imaginatively conceived." *The New York Times*
0-7445-4324-X   £3.99

THE VERY BEST OF AESOP'S FABLES
retold by Margaret Clark, illustrated by Charlotte Voake

Shortlisted for the Kurt Maschler Award, this volume contains eight favourite fables – without the morals.
"Bright as new paint… Clear, snappy and sharp, yet retains all the elegance and point of the originals. Delicately illustrated by the inimitable Charlotte Voake." *The Sunday Times*
0-7445-3149-7   £5.99